# BUBBA GATOR
## & THE GATOR FAMILY
## "No More Hiccups"

Bubba Gator and The Gator Family Books are published by DARBY THE DINOSAUR ENTERPRISES, INC., Grandville, Michigan 49418.

"Hey, Allie, let me down," said Bubba Gator. "It's hot up here and I need a drink of Gator Juice." "Gator Juice," yelled Allie Gator. "Yeah, let's get some Gator Juice." Allie jumped off the teeter-totter.

2

"Yaaagh!" When Allie Gator jumped off Bubba came crashing down.

"Are you okay, Bubba?" asked Big Tooth. "I don't know," said Bubba as he let out a huge *hiccup*. "He's all right," said Allie, "he's just got the hiccups. What we need is some Gator Juice."

The Gators were off to get some Gator Juice. Big Tooth was whistling. Allie Gator was humming a song. Bubba tried to whistle. Then he tried to humm. But all he could do was *hiccup*.

"Boy, this stuff is good," said Big Tooth between slurps. "It's the best stuff in the whole world," said Allie. "Did it make you feel better, Bubba?" asked Big Tooth.

"I feel fine," said Bubba. "but I still-*hiccup*-have the hiccups." Bubba turned all red. "Excuse-*hiccup*-me," he said.

Allie Gator started laughing at Bubba. Big Tooth couldn't help it and he started laughing, too. Pretty soon even Bubba was laughing. Between *hiccups*, that is.

8

"Very funny," said Bubba. "But I still have to do-*hiccup*-something to get rid of these hic-*hiccups*. I know, let's go ask my Grandma for a cure."
"Good idea," said Big Tooth. "She always makes the best cookies."
"Yeah, Cookies!" shouted Allie. "All you guys ever think about is-*hiccup*-your stomachs," said Bubba.

9

"Oh, My!" said Grandma after Bubba blew her glasses off. "Wow, you sure can blow hard, Bubba," said Big Tooth. "Good one!" said Allie. Bubba just *hiccuped*. "I'm sorry it didn't work," said Grandma. "Do you want some cookies?" "Yeah," yelled Allie. "Thanks," said Bubba "Then I'm going home to-*hiccup*-see if my mom can help."

11

Mom and Bubba's little sister, Gita, had a great cure for the hiccups. "All you do is pinch your nose and drink the water," said Gita. Mom pinched her nose and said, "And presto, your hiccups will disappear." She sure sounded funny with her nose pinched.

-HICCUP!

12

"Aw, I got water up my nose," cried Allie. "Man, I'm soaking wet," said Big Tooth. "And I still-*hiccup*- have the hiccups," said Bubba. "Oh well," laughed Mom, "maybe your father can help. He's downstairs."

13

Bubba, Big Tooth and Allie Gator went downstairs to see if Dad could help. They told him the whole story.

14

"I think I may be able to help you boys," said Dad as he looked through his closet.

"Raauuggh!" roared Dad from behind a scary mask. He tried to scare the hiccups out of Bubba. The scaring part worked but Bubba still had the hiccups.

"I can't believe it," said Bubba. "I still-*hiccup*- have the hiccups. Let's go-*hiccup*- back to the playground. Maybe they will just go-*hiccup*-away."

-HICCUP!

17

"Or maybe you will have the hiccups forever, FOR-EV-ER," said Allie Gator. "That would be cool. Introducing Bubba, The Amazing Hiccuping Gator!" "It's not-*hiccup*- funny," said Bubba. "We tried everything, too," said Big Tooth. "Let's go play," said Allie. "Last one there is a rotten gator egg." 18

Bubba was way up in the air again. "I don't know if I -*hiccup*- like it up here," said Bubba. "Don't worry, I won't let you fall again," said Allie. Bubba heard some music coming from the street. "Hey, isn't that the Ice Cream Truck?" he asked.

"ICE CREAM MAN! ICE CREAM MAN!" screamed Allie as he jumped off the teeter-totter. Bubba came crashing down again.

20

"Are you okay?" asked Big Tooth. "Yeah, I guess so," said Bubba. "I must be getting used to it." "Hey," said Allie, "You didn't hiccup." "Hooray!" yelled Bubba. "No more hiccups." "Hooray!" yelled Big Tooth. "No more hiccups." "Hooray!" yelled Allie, "let's get some ice cream."

"It sure is easy eating ice cream when you don't have the hiccups," said Bubba. "You got that right," slurped Big Tooth. "You can-*hiccup*- sure say-*hiccup*-that again," said Allie.

Oh, No!  Now Allie Gator had the hiccups!  "Here we go again," said
Bubba.  "I can't believe it," said Big Tooth.  Allie didn't say anything.
He just *hiccupped*.

# The Author

Ray Russell Bentley was born in Grand Rapids, MI on 11-25-60. He went to Hudsonville High School and studied English at Central Michigan. He makes his home in Grandville, MI with his wife Jodi and their children: Alaina 11, Ritchard 10, T.J. 7, Jake 5 and Morgan 3. Mr. Bentley says, "Reading and writing are the most important skills kids ever learn and Bubba helps make it fun."

# The Illustrator

Timothy J. Gordon was born in Grand Rapids, Michigan on 11-21-69. He graduated from Godwin High School and then attended the Kendall College of Art & Design in Grand Rapids. He is currently employed as an advertising designer with Meijer Inc. Mr. Gordon says, "I hope the books portray a strong sense of family values. It's so important for kids to have a family who cares."

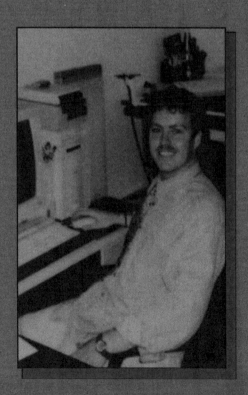